D0578695

Dedicated to my grandmother, Donajean, and my sister, Emily

Copyright © 2020 by Celia Krampien
Published by Roaring Brook Press
Roaring Brook Press is a division of Holtzbrinck Publishing Holdings Limited Partnership
120 Broadway, New York, NY 10271
mackids.com
All rights reserved

Library of Congress Control Number: 2019941022
ISBN: 978-1-250-31660-8

Our books may be purchased in bulk for promotional, educational, or business use. Please contact your
local bookseller or the Macmillan Corporate and Premium Sales Department at (800) 221-7945 ext. 5442 or
by email at MacmillanSpecialMarkets@macmillan.com.

First edition, 2020
Book design by Jen Keenan and Aram Kim
Printed in China by Hung Hing Off-set Printing Co. Ltd., Heshan City, Guangdong Province

10 9 8 7 6 5 4 3 2 1

SUNNY

Celia Krampien

Purchased from
Multnomah County Library
Title Wave Used Bookstore
216 NE Knott St, Portland, OR
503-988-5021

ROARING BROOK PRESS

NEW YORK

Most people do not like rainy days.

Most people would say there is nothing good about trudging to school on a rainy day while the wind crawls up your sleeves and puddles soak your boots, making your footsteps squish and squash.

That is what most people would say.

But not Sunny.
Sunny thought this day was
the perfect day to use her big
yellow umbrella. And it was.

Until a big gust of wind came along.

Now, most people would say that being pulled through the air by an umbrella was a bad sort of situation. But not Sunny, who felt like a bird soaring high above the little town below.

But soon the town below was replaced by a stormy sea.

Now, most people would agree that being blown out to sea was an awful, terrible sort of situation. But not Sunny, who liked watching the white-capped waves rolling and tumbling over one another.

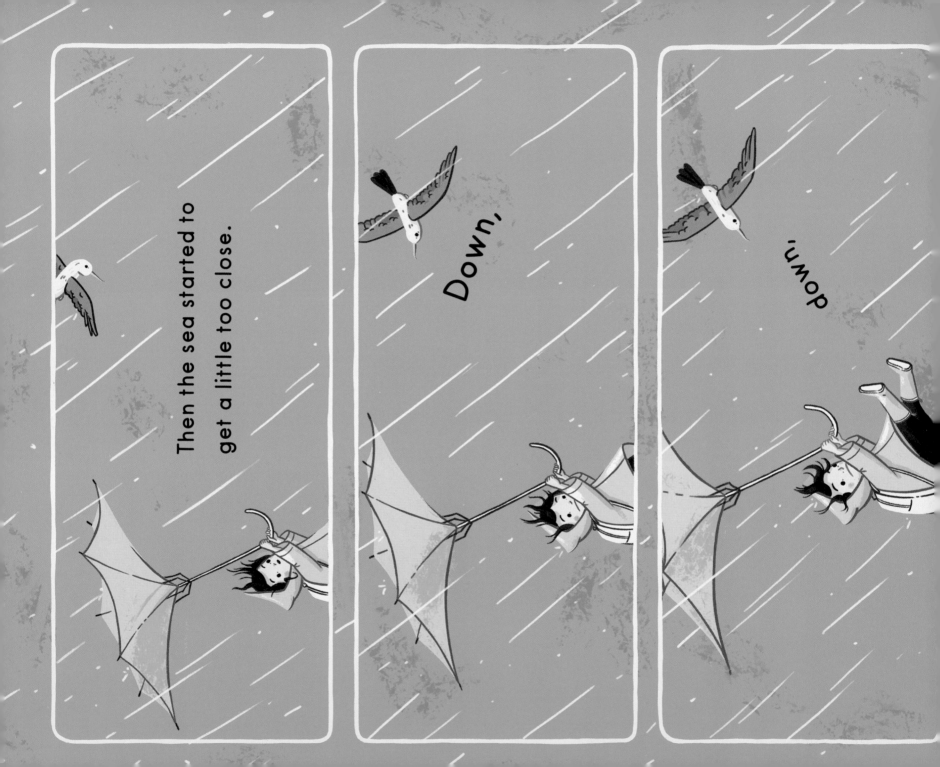

Now, being trapped in a small boat and adrift on a stormy sea is what most people would call a horrible, dreadful, and ghastly sort of situation. But not Sunny, who thought she preferred boating just now to swimming.

That's when the big wave came.

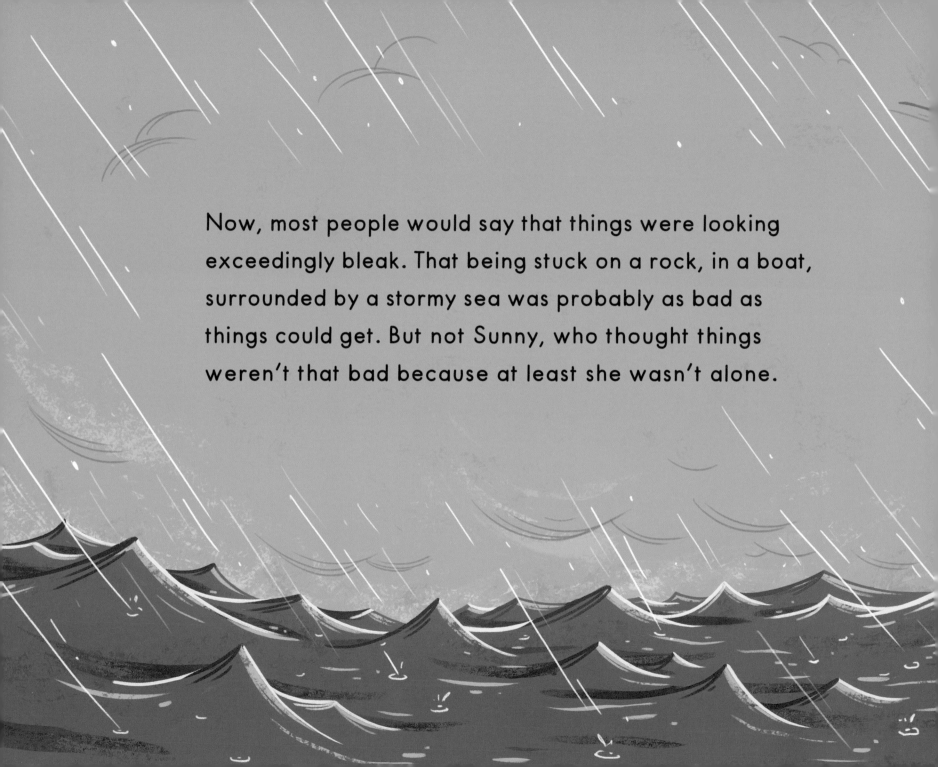

Now, most people would say that things were looking exceedingly bleak. That being stuck on a rock, in a boat, surrounded by a stormy sea was probably as bad as things could get. But not Sunny, who thought things weren't that bad because at least she wasn't alone.

But then she was.

Now, most people would probably cry at this point.

And this time, that's exactly what Sunny did.

But then . . .

Up, up, UP, she rose.
She was lifted off the rock, over a
less-stormy sea, over the little town,

and set down just where she needed to be.
Now, most people would say that being late
for school was a bad kind of situation.

But not Sunny.

She thought that, this one time,
her teacher would understand.

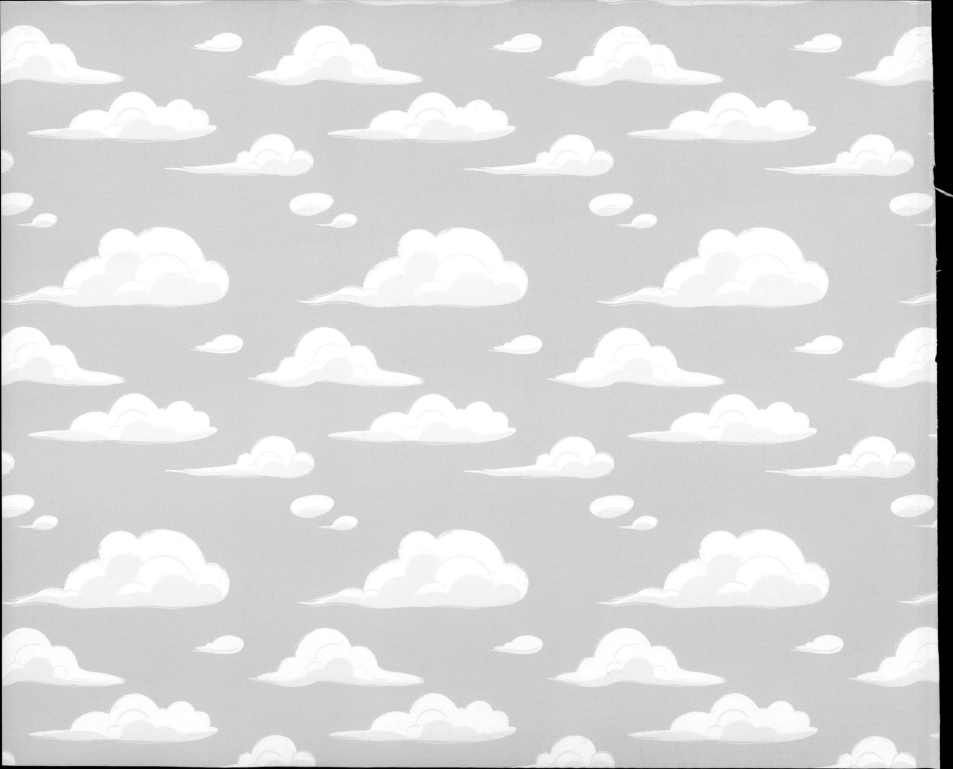